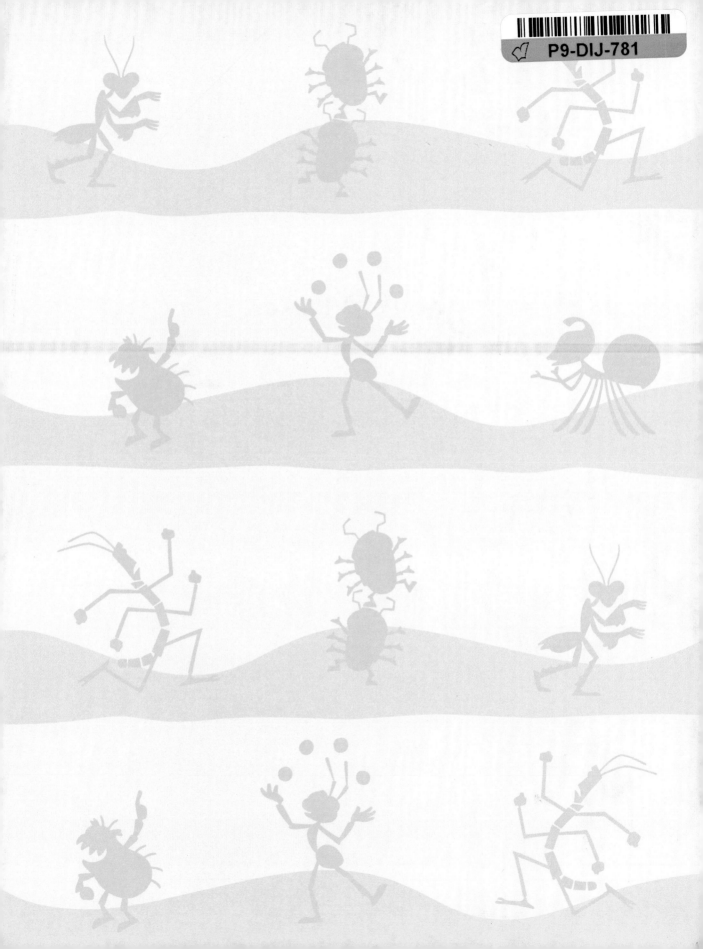

This book belongs to

_____

Flik the Inventor

Published by Advance Publishers
www.advance-publishers.com

Written by Victoria Saxon
Illustrated by Adrienne Brown and Andrew Phillipson
Editorial development and management by Bumpy Slide Books
Illustrations produced by Disney Publishing Creative Development
Cover design by Deborah Boone

ISBN: 1-57973-017-5

Princess Dot and some of the Blueberries stood outside Flik's room in the anthill.

Pop! Wheeeeze! Gulp! came the noises from inside. As always, Flik was trying to invent something to help the ant colony.

"Maybe we should ask him if he needs help," Dot suggested.

But before anyone could answer, there was a loud *thump*! Flik bounced out of the room, landing at Dot's feet.

"Hmmm," Flik muttered as he stood up and brushed himself off. "The flinging mechanism must be too tight."

Flik was so deep in thought he didn't even notice
Dot and her friends. He marched right past them
and back into his room.

"Well," Dot said, "at least we know he's okay."

The next morning, Dot saw Flik at the edge of the fields with a funny-looking machine.

"Hi, Flik!" Dot said. "Whatcha working on?"

"Oh, hello, Princess," said Flik. He smiled happily. "This is my pick-up-and-mover machine."

11

"How does it work?" asked Dot.

"Here, let me show you," Flik said as he helped Dot up onto a rock. Then he started his machine.

Soon an arm on the machine reached out and grabbed Dot! "That tickles!" she said, giggling. Suddenly Dot felt herself being lifted into the air!

A moment later she landed safely on the ground. "Wowee!" cried Dot. "Look how far I moved!" "Excellent!" Flik said. "I'm glad I adjusted that flinging mechanism. Otherwise, you might have ended up on the other side of Ant Island!"

Just then Thorny appeared.

"Flik," Thorny said, "why aren't you collecting food with the rest of the worker ants?"

"Hello, Thorny! I was hoping you'd ask me that very question," Flik replied. "You see, I have invented a new machine. Would you like to see how it works?"

Thorny was angry. "We don't have time for all these silly inventions! There's work to be done! We need to collect food!"

"But—" Flik tried to explain.

"Just get to work like the other ants," Thorny called as he stomped away.

Flik hung his head.

"Don't worry, Flik," Dot said. "You'll figure out some way to use your invention. I just know it."

"Yeah, it must be good for something, but what?" Flik said to Dot as he walked out to the fields to work.

Later that night, Flik sat in his room, trying to think of a useful invention. Suddenly he got an idea. He worked deep into the night.

Early the next morning, Dot found Flik outside looking intently at a large stalk.

"Flik!" she said. "You'd better get out in the fields with the other ants. Thorny's been looking for you!"

"Sure, I will, Dot," Flik said. "But wouldn't you like to see my latest invention first? It's a stalk chopper!"

"Flik, you're gonna get in trouble," Dot warned. "You're supposed to be collecting food."

"Yes, yes," Flik said. "I will, I will. Right after I try this out. Stand back, Princess!"

Flik started up his machine and set to work.

Moments later, the stalk was chopped neatly in half.
"Aha!" Flik cried. "It worked. How do you like
that, Princess?"
But Dot didn't answer. Thorny did.

"How many times do I have to tell you there's work to be done?!" cried Thorny.

"But, Thorny," Flik said, "look at this! It's my new stalk-chopping machine."

"We don't have time for this!" Thorny insisted.

"But I'm sure—" Flik began.

29

"We don't need to chop stalks. We need to collect food!" Thorny told him.

Flik's antennae drooped as he walked out to the fields to join the other worker ants. "That's all Thorny thinks about—harvesting food," Flik mumbled to himself.

Then Flik stopped short.

"That's what we need!" he cried. "A harvester! A machine to collect food!" Flik turned around and raced back to his room.

He looked at his pick-up-and-mover machine. Then he looked at his stalk-chopping machine.

"Hmmm . . . what would happen if I combined them?" Flik thought out loud. "I guess there's only one way to find out!"

The following morning, with his new invention strapped to his back, Flik headed toward the fields. He smiled as he watched two ant children run past him, playing tag. Then he waved to some worker ants collecting food.

Flik sighed happily. He knew that his invention would save the worker ants hours of working time. In fact, Flik thought he might become something of a hero.

Flik tried to get Thorny's attention, but Thorny was too busy talking to Princess Atta. And Princess Dot was nowhere to be found.

"Flik!" one of the worker ants called out. "What crazy thing did you invent this time? Hahaha!"

The other ants laughed, too. "That Flik!" one said. "He's always thinking up useless stuff!"

But Flik didn't mind the other ants' teasing. He was busy starting up his machine. Then he cut down a stalk. Moments later, the flinging mechanism launched dozens of pieces of grain into a basket.

Flik's machine worked!

"Hey!" cried one worker ant. "That's your pick-up-and-mover machine!"

"That's right," Flik said proudly.

"And it's connected to your stalk-chopping machine!" said another ant.

"Uh-huh," Flik replied.

"Wow!" shouted the worker ants.

"Yup. I put them together and made a harvester," Flik explained. "Now one ant can collect as much food as a whole bunch of ants put together!"

"Hooray!" cried the other ants. "Three cheers for Flik!"

Flik grinned. He had done it. He had finally created a really useful machine!

Dear Blueberry Journal,

Boy, the worker ants sure do work hard! Just a few of them collect enough food for the entire ant colony to survive winter. Sometimes the seeds are already on the ground, and the workers pick them up and carry them away in their mouths. Other times they have to cut the seeds off the grasses and weeds before they can take them.

Now that we have Flik's harvester, everyone can gather seeds faster and more easily. Then all the worker ants have to do is carry them inside the nest to keep them dry.

Hooray! More time to play!

Till next time,
Dot